Dear Parents:

Congratulations! Your child is taking the first steps on an exciting journey. The destination? Independent reading!

STEP INTO READING® will help your child get there. The program offers five steps to reading success. Each step includes fun stories and colorful art or photographs. In addition to original fiction and books with favorite characters, there are Step into Reading Non-Fiction Readers, Phonics Readers and Boxed Sets, Sticker Readers, and Comic Readers—a complete literacy program with something to interest every child.

Learning to Read, Step by Step!

Ready to Read   Preschool–Kindergarten
• big type and easy words • rhyme and rhythm • picture clues
For children who know the alphabet and are eager to begin reading.

Reading with Help   Preschool–Grade 1
• basic vocabulary • short sentences • simple stories
For children who recognize familiar words and sound out new words with help.

Reading on Your Own   Grades 1–3
• engaging characters • easy-to-follow plots • popular topics
For children who are ready to read on their own.

Reading Paragraphs   Grades 2–3
• challenging vocabulary • short paragraphs • exciting stories
For newly independent readers who read simple sentences with confidence.

Ready for Chapters   Grades 2–4
• chapters • longer paragraphs • full-color art
For children who want to take the plunge into chapter books but still like colorful pictures.

STEP INTO READING® is designed to give every child a successful reading experience. The grade levels are only guides; children will progress through the steps at their own speed, developing confidence in their reading.

Remember, a lifetime love of reading starts with a single step!

Visit us on the Web!
StepIntoReading.com
randomhouse.com/kids

Educators and librarians, for a variety of teaching tools, visit us at RHTeachersLibrarians.com

ISBN 978-0-385-38508-4 (trade) — ISBN 978-0-385-38509-1 (lib. bdg.)

Printed in the United States of America

10 9 8 7 6 5 4 3 2 1

STEP INTO READING®

2
STEP
READING WITH HELP

Based on the teleplay "Animal School House!"
by Dustin Ferrer
Illustrated by Jason Fruchter

Random House 🏠 New York

The UmiAlarm rings.
Farmer Dan says the
farm is missing two
chickens and four pigs!

One donkey and three
mice are missing, too.

Geo looks with
his Umi Goggles.
The animals are
at the school!

It is time for action!
UmiCar races
to the school.

Geo hears "Oink! Oink!"
in the lunchroom.
The hungry pigs
are inside.

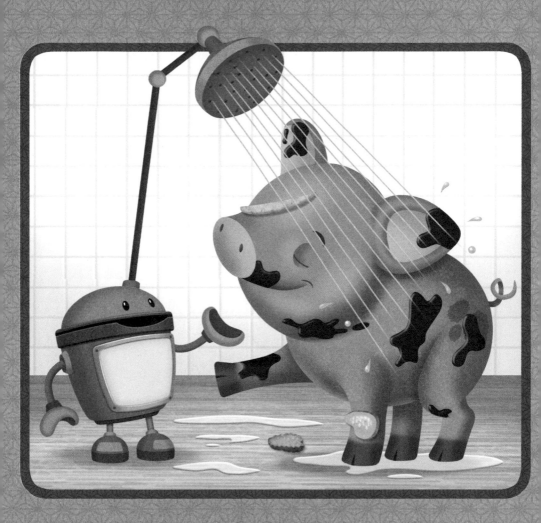

The pigs made
a big mess!
Bot gives them
a shower.

Bok! Bok!

Milli hears the

chickens

in the classroom.

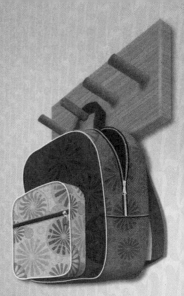

The speedy chickens
move around the room
in a pattern.

Pattern Power!

The pattern is
bookshelf, toys, rug,

bookshelf, toys, rug.

Milli checks the
bookshelf and the toys.
What is next?

Milli finds the chickens
on the rug!

Geo hears

"Squeak! Squeak!"

in the art room.

The silly mice

are painting!

The mice run

and hide.

Bot finds the
mice with his
RoboRadar.

Team Umizoomi hears
the donkey.
The stubborn donkey is
on the playground.

He is on top
of the slide.
He will not
come down.

Super Shapes!

Geo makes ice cream
with a pickle
and french fries on top.

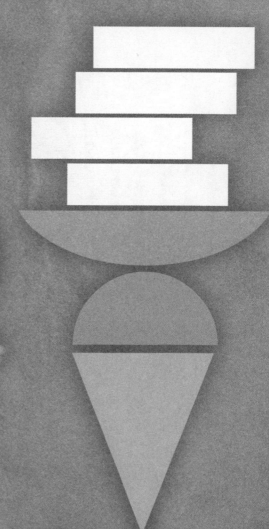

The animals are
back home.
Hooray!
Everybody Crazy Shake!

UmiCar takes them
to the farm.

Team Umizoomi puts
the animals
on a farm wagon.

It is the donkey's
favorite food.
The donkey goes
down the slide.